Especially for Amy Jane, with love
~ M C B

To Basil Bahrani
~ T M

LITTLE TIGER PRESS LTD,
an imprint of the Little Tiger Group
1 Coda Studios, 189 Munster Road,
London SW6 6AW
www.littletiger.co.uk

First published in Great Britain 2010
This edition published 2010

Text copyright © M Christina Butler 2010
Illustrations copyright © Tina Macnaughton 2010
M Christina Butler and Tina Macnaughton have
asserted their rights to be identified as the author
and illustrator of this work under the Copyright,
Designs and Patents Act, 1988

A CIP catalogue record for this book is
available from the British Library

Printed in China

LTP/1800/2848/0719

10 9 8 7 6 5 4 3

The Smiley Snowman

M Christina Butler   Tina Macnaughton

LITTLE TIGER

LONDON

The snowman was nearly finished. Little Bear and Small Fox lifted a big snowball on to his huge body.

"My turn!" cried Fluff Bunny. "Let me help!"

"Come on then, Fluff!" giggled Small Fox. "We can't leave you out!"

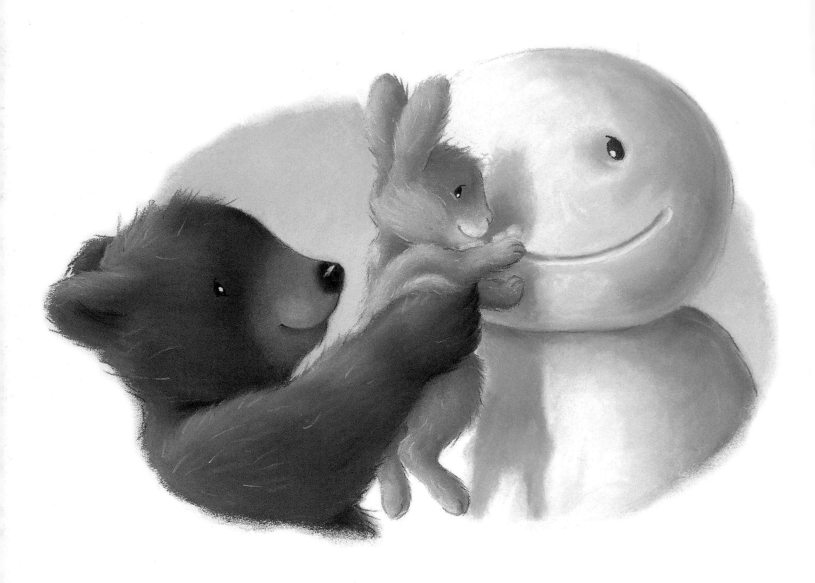

"Here we go!" cried Little Bear, lifting
him up, and Fluff gave the snowman
a great, big smile.

"Yippee!" squeaked Fluff. "He looks
really happy now! Hello, Snowman!"

"Let's go, Fluff!" shrieked Little Bear and
Small Fox, sliding down the hill.
   "But what about Snowman?" Fluff called.
"Don't worry, Snowman, I'll stay with
   you. What shall we play?"

So together they played
snowballs . . .

and Fluff showed the
snowman how to do
headstands.

Then he told stories until
the sky grew dark and
snowflakes began to fall.

One by one, tiny lights started twinkling
in the valley below.

"I have to go now," said Fluff. "Night-
night, Snowman. See you tomorrow!"

Next morning the new snow sparkled bright.
"Wait for me!" gasped Fluff as he bounced
up the hill after Little Bear and Small Fox.
But the snowman looked sad and shivery.

"Oh no!" whispered Fluff. "What's wrong?"

"He looks cold to me," said Little Bear.

"He needs a hat!"

"I'll get a scarf!" cried Small Fox.

And off they went to see what they could find.

"This will warm him up!" giggled Little Bear
as they pulled the woolly hat and scarf
into place.

"What's happened to Fluff?" asked
Small Fox when they'd finished.
"I don't know," replied Little Bear.
"But there's something very strange
coming up the hill! Look!"

"What can it be?" asked Small Fox,
hiding behind Little Bear.
A big, floppy thing with lumpy
bumps was shuffling nearer.
Suddenly Little Bear laughed.
"It's Fluff!" he yelled. "He's got a duvet!
Hold on, Fluff! We're coming!"

Together the friends pulled the duvet
up to the snowman. Then they tucked
it round . . . and pulled it up . . . and
wrapped it round again . . .

until only the snowman's big pebble
eyes were peeping out.

"He'll be nice and cosy now," said
Little Bear. "Come on, Fluff. Small Fox
has got a new sledge!"

Soon they were skimming
down the hill . . .

with snowball fights on the way up — and down they went again — until Fluff was quite tired out and flopped back on the sledge!

"We'll pull you, Fluff," laughed Little Bear. "Let's go and see Snowman."

But something was wrong!

Drip! Drip! Drip! Drops of water were running down the snowman's face, and there were puddles of water everywhere!

"Our snowman's sinking!" Fluff yelled.

"He's melting!" cried Little Bear. "We'll have to make him cold again!"

They pulled off the duvet, and threw his hat and scarf in the air.

"Don't worry, Snowman," cried Fluff. "We'll save you!"

"More snow! More snow!" shouted Little Bear as they padded and packed, and smoothed and patted.

Soon the snowman was bigger
and better than before.
"Wow!" gasped Little Bear.
"We nearly lost him!"
"But why does he still look
so *sad?*" puzzled Fluff, staring
up at the snowman.

Fluff stretched his arms as far as he could
around the snowman's big snow body.
"What's wrong, Snowman?" he asked
gently. "Please don't be so sad."
"Look," whispered Small Fox.
"Something is happening . . ."

"He's smiling!" cried Little Bear suddenly.

"Fluff's done it!" shouted Small Fox.

"Snowman wasn't cold on the outside.
He was cold on the inside!" Fluff grinned.
"He just needed a hug!"

And as the stars twinkled in the clear
night sky, they gave the snowman another
hug and his happy smile grew bigger
than ever!

This Little Tiger book belongs to:

Elie